P9-DFX-507

Sophie Peterman

tells the

Truth!

Sarah Weeks

Illustrated by
Robert Neubecker

BEACH LANE BOOKS
New York   London   Toronto   Sydney

For Jim Fyfe, with love—S. W.

For my girls: Ruthie, Izzy, and Joey—R. N.

BEACH LANE BOOKS

An imprint of Simon & Schuster Children's Publishing Division

1230 Avenue of the Americas, New York, New York 10020

Text copyright © 2009 by Sarah Weeks

Illustrations copyright © 2009 by Robert Neubecker

BEACH LANE BOOKS is a trademark of Simon & Schuster, Inc.

For information about special discounts for bulk purchases,

please contact Simon & Schuster Special Sales at 1-866-506-1949 or business@simonandschuster.com.

The Simon & Schuster Speakers Bureau can bring authors to your live event.

For more information or to book an event, contact the Simon & Schuster Speakers Bureau at 1-866-248-3049

or visit our website at www.simonspeakers.com.

Book design by Lauren Rille

The text for this book is set in Bodoni.

The illustrations for this book are rendered in India ink

on watercolor paper and then colored digitally.

Manufactured in China

First Edition

2 4 6 8 10 9 7 5 3 1

Library of Congress Cataloging-in-Publication Data

Weeks, Sarah.

Sophie Peterman tells the truth! / Sarah Weeks ; illustrated by Robert Neubecker.—1st ed.

p. cm.

Summary: A disgruntled big sister reveals unpleasant facts about babies.

ISBN: 978-1-4169-8686-7 (hardcover : alk. paper)

[1. Babies—Fiction. 2. Brothers and sisters—Fiction. 3. Humorous stories.] I. Neubecker, Robert, ill. II. Title.

PZ7.W42235Sr 2009

[E]—dc22

2008051058

My name is Sophie Peterman, and I am here to tell you that if your parents ever ask, "WOULD YOU LIKE TO HAVE A LITTLE BROTHER OR SISTER SOMEDAY?" you should definitely say . . .

That's what **I** should have said three years ago when my mom and dad brought my little brother home from the hospital. **EVERYBODY** came over to see him.

"Look at his **TEENY-TINY** fingernails! Aren't they sweet?"

"Look at his **EENSY-WEENSY** little toes. Aren't they precious?"

"What a cute **WITTLE ITTY-BITTY** baby. **GITCHY-GITCHY-GITCHY-GOO!**"

What was wrong with these people? Were they **NUTS?**

My name is
SOPHIE PETERMAN,
and I am here
to tell you the

TRUTH!

Babies are not sweet.

Babies are not precious.

Babies are not cute.

Babies are . . .

Here are some true things about babies:

1. If you try to sell one, nobody will buy it.

2. If you try to

pick one up,

BEWARE,

they leak.

3. When babies eat

you don't want to watch.

At first, babies are like

ALIENS,

They have big eyes and
bald heads, and they sit
around all day making
strange noises.

Then, when babies learn to crawl,
they are like **PIRATES.**

They come into your room uninvited and

dig for treasure in your underwear drawer.

And when they talk, it's impossible to understand
what they mean.

But the worst thing is when babies learn to walk.
That's when they become . . .

Here are some true things about monsters:

1. A monster always
   wants whatever you have.

2. If you don't give a
   monster what he
   wants, he will scream.

3. If you pinch a screaming monster even the tiniest
little bit, the monster's mother will come running in,
and you will end up with nothing—

ZIPPO,

NADA,

ZILCH.

In case **YOU** ever have to live with a monster,
here is some advice:

If you have to sit next to a monster all the way to your aunt and uncle's house in Syracuse, New York,

DO NOT BREATHE IN THROUGH YOUR NOSE.

If you are taking a bath with a monster
and you notice extra bubbles . . .

GET OUT!

And if a monster accidentally swallows your
lucky marble when you're not looking, you
can expect to get it back in about three days.
But you will never, EVER, want to touch it again.

EVER.

NOW PAY ATTENTION,

because this is the most important part of all:

If your monster starts smiling and
clapping his pudgy little hands
whenever he sees you . . .

and if he starts calling you
something really cute because
he can't say your name right . . .

and he only wants *you* to feed him, and he
always cries when you go off to school . . .

You might actually

start to **LIKE** him.

And if that happens,
no matter what,

DO
NOT
TELL
YOUR
PARENTS.

Because if you do, they'll bring home another one.
And then . . .

you'll
be
OUTNUMBERED.

My name is

SOPHIE PETERMAN,

and I am telling you the truth.